FEBRUARY IS FOR FORD
MOUNTAIN MEN OF MUSTANG MOUNTAIN

KACI ROSE

Copyright © 2023, by Kaci Rose, Five Little Roses Publishing. All Rights Reserved.

No part of this publication may be reproduced, distributed, or transmitted in any form or by any means, including photocopying, recording, or other electronic or mechanical methods, or by any information storage and retrieval system without the prior written permission of the publisher, except in the case of very brief quotations embodied in critical reviews and certain other noncommercial uses permitted by copyright law.

Publisher's Note: This is a work of fiction. Names, characters, places, and incidents are a product of the author's imagination.

Locales and public names are sometimes used for atmospheric purposes. Any resemblance to actual people, living or dead, or to businesses, companies, events, institutions, or locales is completely coincidental.

Book Cover By: Kelly Lambert-Greer

Editing By: Debbe @ On The Page, Author and PA Services

To the Match of the Month Patrons, especially...

Jackie Ziegler

Thank you so much for your support. We couldn't do what we love without you!

GET FREE BOOKS!

Do you like Military Men? Best friends brothers? What about sweet, sexy, and addicting books?

If you join Kaci Rose's Newsletter you get these books free!
https://www.kacirose.com/free-books/

Now on to the story!

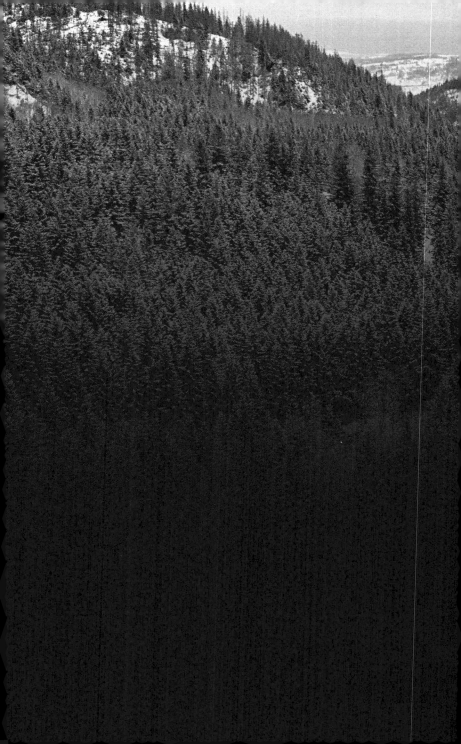

CHAPTER 1
FORD

WHAT IN THE HELL?

Of course, I'd be "Mr. February." I should have seen that coming with my name starting with "F" and with Ruby having so much success with Jackson. Or at least claiming that Jackson's relationship with Emma is because of her.

My guess is if we can't put a stop to her before next month then Miles will be next.

"Daddy, why do you look like you just ate a lemon?" my daughter Isabella asks.

"It's an adult thing, Izzy," I tell her, staring at the ad Ruby has put up on the visitor Bureau website.

"Dad, I'm a whole five years old! Tell me the truth I can handle it," she says as she holds up five fingers. She cocks her head to the side and her adorable curly pigtails frame her face.

It's true my daughter is an old soul and much more

mature than other kids her age growing up out here the way she has on the mountain.

"Let's just say Ruby is up to her shenanigans again and this time I'm caught in the crossfires," I tell her.

"Oh, you mean the flyers with your face on them I saw them when we came into the diner. I already know. I told you I'm five." She actually rolls her eyes at me and I start to wonder if I'm going to be able to handle her in another five years.

I don't know if I should respond to the eye-rolling or the fact that there are flyers up around town with my face on them and thankfully I don't have to decide because my phone rings.

After checking the caller ID, I answer. I don't get many phone calls except for a few people, so I'm not surprised to find it to be my best friend, Luna.

We've been best friends since we were little, and even now she's Izzy's kindergarten teacher, which makes things easy unless Izzy tries to take advantage of the situation which she has done multiple times this year already.

"Hello?"

"Ford. My house has been broken into!" A panicked Luna greets me from the other end of the line.

"Luna, calm down. What do you mean your house has been broken into?" I raise my voice which of course caches Jackson's attention. He looks over at me, his brows arched.

"Someone threw a rock through my window and

my stuff is all over the place inside." She sounds like she is on the verge of tears.

My pulse skyrockets. If anyone hurts her, they will have to deal with me. "Fuck. Get back in your car and lock the door. Call the police. I'm leaving the diner now and will be there in just a few minutes."

Looking over at Izzy, I know that my cussing has gotten her attention. She's looking at me with curious eyes now and I try to smile, but I know it's not going to help, my daughter knows me all too well.

Jackson has covered the distance to the door in a few long strides. "I'm going with you."

"Emma can stay here with me and Izzy while you boys go take care of Luna." Ruby shoos us out the door, but not before Jackson pulls Emma close for a kiss.

"First Ruby's hare-brained scheme and now a break-in. What the hell is happening to Mustang Mountain?" I didn't wait for an answer. The sooner I could get to Luna, the better I'd feel.

Even though I hate to hang up with her, I have to so I can call the other guys Miles and Asher.

First up is Miles, "Luna just called. Her house has been broken into. We need to get over there and help her get it squared away for the night."

I don't have to ask him about helping Luna. Because I know whatever he's doing he's going to drop it.

"On it. I'll call Asher too." He says before we hang up.

As I pull into Luna's drive, I am the first one there.

I barely get my car in park when she jumps out of her car and heads toward me. She walks right into my arms, and I hold her there, relieved to know she is okay.

While she takes comfort in my arms, I survey the front of her house. The front door is cracked open and the window on the front porch is shattered. There is glass all over the porch and her curtains are blowing in the breeze right out the window.

"Have you gone inside?" I ask.

"No. I saw the door and the window before I even stepped foot on the porch, then called you."

"Okay, the guys should be here any moment and we will take a look around."

Not a minute later, the roar of Asher's diesel truck fills the air coming down the street and Jackson is right behind him.

"Miles is grabbing some wood to board up the windows. He will be right behind us," Asher says as he looks over the front of the house.

"Stay with her while we will go clear the house," Jackson says and I nod.

Best to make sure no one is still in there. Though we are all hoping we don't find anyone because right now I don't think Luna can handle it.

Asher follows Jackson in, and Luna and I wait. Miles pulls up in with wood in the back of his truck just as Asher and Jackson walk out of the house.

"Whoever it was is long gone. We need to call the police before we touch anything." Asher says as he pulls out his phone.

He will handle it, and I know we don't have to worry about it. It doesn't seem very long before a deputy shows up and it's Asher's friend Sean. Before walking toward the house, he greets them. Then they spend a few minutes inside as Luna watches on, still not having moved from my side.

"Ma'am, will you come walk through and see if anything is missing so I can write an official report?" Sean steps back onto the porch.

"Yeah. Umm Ford, you will come with me, right?" Her voice is a little shaky.

"Of course. I won't leave your side. Come on." I take her hand and lead her into the house.

We walk room by room, starting with the living room. Every door is open, the drawers, everything was thrown around, and there are broken picture frames holding her photos. Moving on to the kitchen even though the cabinet is open, food is thrown around, and milk is even spilled on the floor. Her back door is wide open as well. Chairs are turned over in the dining room.

"So far, nothing looks missing. Just destroyed." She says as we move to the hallway.

The guest bedroom dresser has every drawer pulled out and tossed on the floor, the hall bath has towels thrown on the ground and they ripped the shower curtain off and tossed it in the tub.

Luna seemed unfazed until we got to her room and it was in just as bad of shape. Her clothes are everywhere, her bed sheets were ripped off and on the floor, and they threw everything off every surface on to the floor.

She leaves my side and runs to her nightstand.

"No, no, no. NO!" Luna shouts as she goes through her nightstand drawer, or what is left of it.

She pulls out the wood box I've seen her always have with her and opens it.

"No!" She shouts again. Then she drops to her knees and looks frantically under the bed and nightstand.

Walking over to her, I gently pull her up off the ground before she cuts herself on any broken glass.

"Luna. What's missing?" I ask softly.

"My grandmother's wedding ring. It was the only thing of value I own." She starts crying.

I remember that ring. She wore it for days when her grandmother died. It was the only thing that would calm her during that time. I remember her telling me over and over that when she got married that was the ring she was going to wear.

As a teenager, I'd picture that, and it would be me she'd be marrying. Crazy, I know, but I feel this loss as if it's part of my future gone too.

Then I help her file a police report and find a photo of the ring on her phone. The guys stand guard and answer questions as needed. Once the police officer leaves, the guys take over.

"Let's get the place secured and boarded up," Asher says.

"I'll help." Miles follows him out the front door.

"She can't stay here," Jackson says.

"I know. Luna packs up any valuables and some clothes and come stay with me." I tell her softly, trying to give her directions without making her panic.

"Why can't I stay here? They said they are securing the place," she says picking up clothes from the floor.

I make a mental note to make sure they all get washed because I hate the idea of some stranger handling things that will touch her skin.

"They can put wood up, but it won't stop the cold. This house won't stay warm and I can't have you freezing to death. Besides, the wood won't stop someone if they plan to come back and want to get in. They can just go through another window," Jackson says.

I glare at him and he just shrugs his shoulders. Everything he says is true, but it could have been said with more finesse.

But I know Luna will listen to Jackson's thoughts because the three of us went to school together and Jackson was always the voice of reason among us. He still is.

"Ok," she agrees and goes to her closet to get a suitcase.

Jackson and I help her pack up clothes, toiletries, and stuff for work. Miles and Asher help load it into my truck. Once they are done, we make sure everything is locked up.

"We will get someone out here to clean this up so

she doesn't have to worry about it," Miles says once we are finished and Luna is in my truck.

"Thanks. Once the shock wears off, she will start making a list of things to do and I will see what we can help her with," I tell them.

"I'll follow you back. Emma took Izzy back to your place." Jackson says as we head out.

Once we are in the car, and on our way, Luna speaks again.

"Where is Izzy?" she asks. Her voice sounds small and miles away.

Damn. I've been so worried about Luna and getting her settled that I haven't had time to think about what I'm going to tell my daughter.

Izzy won't let the fact that her teacher is sleeping in our guest room go unnoticed.

CHAPTER 2
LUNA

TODAY IS one of the worst days I've ever had in my life.

When I got home from work, I thought it couldn't get any worse and bam there is everything in my house torn through by some stranger. The most important thing in the world to me is gone. As we drive up the mountain, I'm numb and can't feel anything.

It's slow going due to the snow and the mountain is closed except for residents. All the guys up here have massive trucks and snow plows and everything they need to live off their land because they are happy to be snowed in for months at a time.

Ford is one of them. Since we were young, he's been my best friend, and I knew for years that he'd always ended up out here. I stayed in town because I like being close to the school, close to work, and the idea of living out here by myself just didn't appeal to me.

Now it's the only place I want to be. Away from everything, all my problems, and safe with the one person I can count on for anything. As we pull into his house, the fireplace is giving off smoke and the lights are on.

With the snow on the ground, it almost looks like one of those picturesque postcards. The ones that make living in a cabin in the mountains look like something from a magazine.

"Come on, let's get your settled and get Izzy to bed so you can have some time to process it all," Ford says.

"I don't even begin to know where to start processing everything. It's not just the break in. It was a bad day at work and just everything." Leaning my head back against the headrest, I close my eyes for just a moment.

Tomorrow won't be much better because I have to go in and break my kids' hearts and that is even more stressful than having my house broken into and torn apart.

"Let's go. I've got your stuff," Ford says. His voice is soft and reassuring. I know he will always have my back.

With what little strength I have left, I step out of his truck and paste on a fake smile for Izzy's sake. The last thing I need is to worry her, and I don't know how much Ford wants her to know.

"Luna!" Izzy squeals as soon as we walk through the door.

She runs up and hugs me. Her little arms squeeze

me so tight they seem to squeeze tears from my eyes. Of course, that's the moment I lose it.

By the time she pulls away, tears are running down my face and I can't stop them.

"Oh, girl, come here." Emma hugs me and then guides me to the couch.

"I knew it was a matter of time before it all hit you," Ford says.

"It's not just the break in. It's the ring, and it's having to cancel the kids Valentine's Day party because no one volunteered to help. Tomorrow I have to break their little hearts and I just can't," I cry.

Of course, Izzy hears it all. When Ford pulls me into his arms again, I realize it's my safe place. I can hear Izzie's wheels turning.

"Daddy, you can help with the party, right? Please, I know we can't help with the house, but we can do this, and it might take her mind off everything." Izzy whispers the last part like it's some secret.

For is rubbing my back and I know he won't answer right away. He's always one to think things through. Honestly, though, I expect him to say no. Ford is a great dad, one of the best I know, but he really isn't a kid person, especially around fifteen other kids.

"Would you be able to still do the party if I were to help?" He asks in my ear so only I can hear.

"Yes," I tell him.

He takes a deep breath and blows it out.

"Okay. I'll help then." He says, shocking me.

Taking a step back, I just stare at him.

"Are you sure? This means helping around the kids..." I say skeptically. I want to make sure he knows what he's getting himself into.

"I'm sure." He says in his no nonsense voice. And I know there's no point in arguing with him.

"Do you need help with snacks or food? I'm more than happy to bake and bring something in for the kids," Emma says.

"That would actually be great! Anything Valentine themed, and pink or red would be great."

"Oh, I found some of the cutest kids' snacks online that are for Valentine's Day, and I can't wait to make them. How many kids are in your class?" Emma gushes.

"18," I tell her.

"Don't forget the other teachers," Izzy adds. "They're always in and out of the classroom all day."

"I will definitely make extras. Jackson is waiting in the driveway for me, so I'm going to leave now. You two have a good night and call if you need anything at all." Emma says before giving me a big hug and then heading out the door.

"This is going to be so much fun. It's going to be like having a sleepover. I bet I'm the only kid in my class that gets a sleepover with my teacher." Izzy says excitedly, jumping up and down full of excitement.

"Well, it's some extraordinary circumstances when you've known your teacher since the day you were born. Now, go upstairs and get ready for bed," Ford says.

"Can Luna read me my book tonight?" she asks as she bounces towards the staircase.

Ford looks at me and I know he's wondering if I'm in the mood for it.

"That's fine. I'll just make it a short book." I tell her and her whole face lights up.

"You don't have to read to her. I can do it if you just want to stay down here and relax," Ford says.

"No, I don't want her worried about me. If I do this, then she'll be more focused on the sleepover aspect than anything else," I say.

He understands and follows me upstairs. She's all smiles and giggles as we tuck her into bed and read her a story. She even tries to get a second story out of the deal, but I know how she works. One more story leads to two more and then three more and she'll be up way past her bedtime.

Once back downstairs, we both collapse on the couch. I love that girl but it takes a lot of energy to keep up being fake excited in the midst of everything that happened today.

"Have you eaten dinner?" Ford asks once he joins me in the living room.

Honestly, I had to stop to think because I don't remember the last time I ate. Lunchtime maybe?

"No, I haven't," I tell him honestly.

He nods, then goes into the kitchen and pulls out what I'm sure are leftovers and heats them up for me. Even though both my mind and body are exhausted, my mind is racing, and I couldn't sleep if I tried right now. It's a very odd feeling.

Ford brings me a plate of spaghetti and some leftover garlic bread that Emma made Izzy and sits down on the couch to eat with me.

"Tomorrow, the guys and I will go back and look at the house to see if we can find any clues. We will also work on getting the place cleaned up again and getting the window fixed." He says as we start eating.

"I feel like I should tell you not to worry about it and I will handle all that, but to be honest I'm just too exhausted to fight you on it," I sigh.

"Good. Because you'd lose the fight anyway," he says.

Though I almost considered calling out of work for tomorrow, but we have too much to do for the party and I need to stay busy to keep my mind off everything.

Even so, I'm pretty sure I could sleep for the next year and still feel this tired in the morning.

"Come on, let's get you to bed," Ford says, taking my plate.

I hadn't even realized I was starting to drift off.

CHAPTER 3
FORD

AFTER SEEING Luna off to work and Izzy off to school, I'm heading to meet the guys at Luna's house. We have a lot of work to do, just cleaning up and fixing the window and some of the doors. Not to mention trying to find any clue who did this and figure out a game plan to get her grandmother's ring back.

I'm the first guy there and when I pull up, I find Hades asleep on the front porch. He raises his head and studies me as I reach into my glove box and pull out one of the peanut butter canola bars that I have stashed there.

Izzy makes me carry them for times like this when I run in to Hades. She loves to feed him. Right now I feel like he knew Luna's house needed to be guarded and I want to make sure to reward him for doing just that.

Walking up to the porch, I sit down on the porch steps. Though he's still on guard, Hades gets up and comes over to lay down right beside me. Even laying down his head, it's about an inch taller than mine as I sit here.

Unwrapping the granola bar, I hold it out in my hand and he gently picks it up and chews it. As he eats, he lets me pet him. I remember when Jackson rescued him as a pup. Hades maybe all wolf, but he's gentle and protective of everyone in this town.

His fur isn't soft like your everyday dog is. But he loves being petted and scratched behind the ears. Though he likes the attention on his own terms. So when he's done eating, he gets up and stretches before going down the stairs.

When Jackson pulls up, he walks over to say hi to Jackson and then runs off to the woods behind Luna's house.

"He was here when I got here. It looked like he had spent the night on the porch. I gave him one of the peanut butter granola bars Izzy makes me carry for him," I tell Jackson.

"He has a knack for knowing where he's needed. And how to sucker food out of people," he says to me with a smile as Miles and Asher pull up.

"How's Luna doing?" Jackson asks.

"She insisted on going to work today, even though I tried to get her to stay home. She's exhausted and stressed but trying to put on a brave face," I tell them.

"Do we have a list of suspects?" Asher asks.

"I was thinking about this last night. There's only a few people that I can really put on to a list. One being her ex because he was always asking to borrow money.

If we're thinking it might be a stalker thing, there's a persistent dad at her school that keeps asking her out and flirting even though she keeps turning him down and asking him to stop." I tell them while wracking my brain to see if I missed anyone.

"There is the slight chance whoever broke into her house is somehow tied to Ruby's profile on me. Everyone in town knows how close we are. I don't want to rule anything out just yet," I add on.

"There is a new guy in town. Ruby mentioned something about him being ex-military. But other than that, no one really knows anything about him. He only showed up in town about two days ago," Miles says.

"It's probably just a coincidence, but let's look into him just to be safe" "Alright then, let's go through the house and see if we can find any clues that we might have missed yesterday. And let's make a note of anything that needs to be fixed up so that we can get Luna back in here as soon as possible," Jackson says as we all go into the house.

Somehow, the place seems worse than I remember it from last night. Entering the house, we decide to split up. I headed for her bedroom. While I trust these guys with my life, I don't really want them touching her clothes and more personal objects. I put her sheets on the bed, and then slowly pick up her clothes, making a pile of them on the bed as well.

Something strikes me as odd. The entire house has been trashed, but things like her dresser haven't really been gone through. If someone was looking for an easy target, then they'd have gotten in, took the TV and left. Or they might have gone right to the bedroom for the jewelry, but it's almost like they were trying to cover their tracks, or maybe getting revenge.

The guys and I have seen much worse. Any time we can, we help women out of bad situations. It's part of what our Motorcycle Club is, even if in the winter we opt to drive our trucks instead of our bikes.

Even though, we like our quiet lives, we like helping people and animals too. So, I'm not just shooting from the hip when I sense something seems off. Thankfully, I'm not the only one that notices it.

"So, we have the window in the living room that has to be repaired," Jackson says.

"The closet door in the office will have to be repaired too," Asher says.

"The kitchen and dining room is just a mess but I don't think there's anything that will have to really be fixed," Miles says.

"From the looks of it, there aren't any repairs needed in the bedroom. But something about all of this just seems off," I tell them.

"I agree. Things haven't really been gone through. It's more of a mess was deliberately made than anything," Asher says.

"Let me take some measurements on the window and door. I can head to the hardware store later and see if I can find one without having to special order anything," Jackson says.

"I'll talk to Ruby, Miles says. "Maybe the girl who

cleans her cabins would be able to come in and help us get this cleaned up for Luna."

"Why don't we each take one of the men I mention earlier and look into them? I'll take her ex because I know what he looks like and have a possible lead on where he might be," I tell them.

"Let me know who the dad at the school is and I'll look into him," Miles says.

"I've seen the new guy in town before and I think I know where I can find him. So, I'll take him. Also, make sure to send us each a photo of the ring so we know what to look for," Jackson says.

"Then I'll ask around in town, starting with Ruby to see if we're missing any possible suspects. But I'll make sure to drive home the coincidence of the timing of the break in with her profile on you. Maybe this is enough to get her to stop. I doubt it, but the rest of us can hope," Asher shakes his head.

We all know asking Ruby about something is like asking to hear one of the world's longest stories on the subject. Even though she means well, she likes to talk, and on something like this she's going to want to make sure that no detail is missed.

"Sounds good. Let me know whatever you hear. I know Luna is going to want updates as much as possible." With that everyone agrees and heads out.

Once I get home, I start doing some digging on her ex. The easiest way to track him down is through good old social media. With Luna staying here, she wasn't able to bring her car up the mountain, so I had to take her to work today, which was no big deal because I also had to take Izzy into school.

That also means that I can pick them up a little later because Izzy will stay with Luna after school until she's ready for me to come get them. Izzy was so excited about that because she thinks it's this super-secret cool after school club. I'm sure she was telling everyone in her class about it too.

> Luna: Hey we're ready whenever you're able to come get us. Izzy is having a blast, so don't feel rushed.
>
> Me: on my way.

I've learned some days Luna has a lot going on after class and after school and other days she leaves not too long after the kids do. But this week she's staying to make sure she gets everything done for the Valentine's Day party.

I headed into town and park at the school and decide to go to her classroom to make sure that they didn't need any help bringing anything home. The school has pretty good security, but I went to the school as a kid and grew up in this town and they all know me so they don't even bother me as I go into the building.

The door to Luna's classroom is open and when I peek in I find my daughter's cleaning up one of the tables. She's putting away a bunch of pink and red paper, so I'm guessing she was helping with something Valentine's Day related.

"Do you two need any help?" I ask stepping into the room.

"Nope we got this Daddy," Izzy says in her sweet little voice as she finishes putting her stuff away.

When I look over at Luna, she offers me a smile.

"I could use some help with that box on my desk. We're going to take that and do a few things at home after dinner," she says.

It's almost like a punch in the gut. All this is so natural. Her with my daughter, no one giving a second thought about her coming back to my house, or about her calling it home.

There's no doubt in my mind that our house could use a woman's touch, it's been Izzy and I from the start. Her mother and I never had a real relationship and she never wanted kids.

Originally, the plan had been for us to share custody of Izzy, and we had it all worked out. The moment I held her in my arms that day at the hospital, I was in love with Izzy. But while a parental switch went on for me that day, it seemed to flip off for her mother.

A few weeks later, she signed her rights saying she wanted nothing to do with the baby. Then she moved away and there's been not a word from her since.

Luna was my biggest supporter. That was the only other time she stayed at my house. Not only did she help me get on my feet, but she learned how to take care of a baby because I had no clue what I was doing. Even then, it felt right having her there.

She and Izzy share a special bond. One I imagine is pretty darn close to a mother and daughter, with a side of best friends.

"So we need to stop at the market and do some shopping. While we're there, I was thinking we could grab pizza for dinner." I tell them and Izzy jumps up and down.

"Yes! pizza sounds sooo good right now," Izzy squeals.

"I guess we are overruled. Pizza it is," Luna jokes.

Once we are in the car, I have to remind myself that all this is just temporary because it feels like more than that, it feels like a little family.

CHAPTER 4
LUNA

IT'S PRETTY obvious how excited Izzy is for this Valentine's Day party. We had pizza for dinner and the moment we walked in the house, she was ready to start helping with all the Valentine's Day crafts we have to do for decorations. She was even able to wrangle her dad in to help.

There's something kind of comical watching a big mountain man like Ford cutting out pink hearts and covering them in glitter. Izzy thinks so too because she hasn't stopped giggling the whole time.

For once, it was so nice not to come home to an empty house. Growing up I always thought having my own place was going to be this big magical thing, but no one tells you how horrible it is coming home day after day to an empty house.

But coming home to Ford and Izzy? It's like walking into a house full of life- walking into a home. I've always loved kids and knew I wanted to be a mom but it wasn't until today that I realized how badly I truly craved a family of my own.

Not that I have any prospects for dating, nor am I anywhere close to being able to create that family, but it's definitely moving up on the priority list. I love my job, and the kids and people that I deal with on a regular basis. Now it's time to make the next stage of my life a priority. But that's all things that can be dealt with later, after my life settles back down.

For now, I'll just enjoy my best friend and his daughter who is also like a best friend to me.

"So, is this what you do at home after school every night?" Ford asks.

"Kind of. When we have a holiday coming up, I'll set up the decorations. Then I'll work on getting all the assignments ready for the next day and the following week. I'll go over and review papers and make sure everyone's on track, that sort of thing. Usually, I put on the TV while I do it because I don't normally have someone to keep me company," smiling at them.

We spend the next hour or so working on the decorations, while Ford asked me questions about my job, the school, my class, and things like that. Izzy jumps in and answers questions when she can.

Ford even asks her questions remembering her friend's names or the names of kids she's talked about in the past. It's really sweet to see how much attention he really pays to her and the things that she says.

"Alright Princess, it's time to get ready for bed," Ford says as we wrap up the decorations.

"But Dad!" Izzy starts to whine.

"No buts, you have school tomorrow. Let's go," he says but his tone is soft and gentle.

"Can you and Luna read me a book tonight?" She pouted a little, and it's cute but I know she's overtired as it's been a really long day.

"How about we read you a book together?" I suggest and her eyes light up.

"I know just the one! Daddy can read the prince part and you can read the Princess part!" She jumps up and runs upstairs excited again about going to bed.

"Once she's all set up and in bed, we'll talk about my visit with the guys today," Ford whispers as if his daughter could hear us all the way upstairs.

I smile and nod my head, but it's like a bucket of cold ice water. Until now I've been able to put the break in out of my mind, and simply enjoy my time here.

When Izzy was done brushing her hair and teeth and all changed into her PJs, we headed upstairs. We find her in bed with the book she wants us to read in her lap.

I'm used to reading books to kids. I do it every day at work. It's pretty much part of my job description as being a kindergarten teacher. But I never knew how much fun it would be to read a book with Ford. He gets all into it with the voices and his one goal is to make the both of us laugh.

After we are done with the book and we tuck her into bed, I'm pretty sure she is going to fall asleep with a smile on her face. I love that feeling of making that little girl happy.

When we go downstairs, we sit on the couch and Ford wastes no time in pouring me a glass of wine and handing it to me. I have a feeling whatever he has to say, I'm not going to like it.

"So I met with the guys are your place this morning after I dropped you girls off. Hades was there on the front porch almost like he knew the place needed guarding overnight. I fed him and he was on his way." He says his golden brown eyes sparkle at the memory.

Izzy loves Hades as if he was her own personal pet and insists her dad feeds him every time he sees him. She's even made him buy Hades a few toys to give him. I'm not sure what he does with the toys, but we like to think he takes him to his den wherever that is.

"Then we went through the house looking for more clues. The window and an inside door are all that seem to need to be fixed. Otherwise, it's just a lot of cleaning. We didn't find any clues, though we do have a list of suspects." He says, but doesn't meet my eyes.

I've known him for so long I can tell he isn't telling me something, but I also trust him. If it's something he doesn't want to tell me, then I'm not sure it's something I want to know.

"Who is on the list?" I ask.

"Your ex, Burce. That dad that keeps bugging you at school, and the new guy in town. No one knows much about him but he showed up a day before your house was broken in to so we want to check him out too. Is there anyone else who should be on the list?" he asks.

"Not that I can think of. I wouldn't even have thought about the guy at school. He seems like such a nice guy, just maybe a little lonely," I shrug.

This guy's kid isn't in my class thankfully, but he makes it a point to stop by and check on me once a week and ask if I have changed my mind on going out with him. I assure him I haven't and wish him well.

But I complain to Ford about it because he never hides the fact that he's checking me out and it creeps me out. I brought an extra coat to the school and kept it on the back of my chair and put it on when he showed up. Even though I know it's silly, it's just an extra layer between me and his eyes.

"Better to leave no stone unturned, Luna. We divided up each suspect and I'm looking into Bruce," he says.

"What have you found?"

"Nothing. I found him on social media, but he's pretty much dropped off the face of the earth about three weeks ago. He lost his job, and no one has heard from him. On the flip side, there is no sign of him in town either."

Great. Even though I didn't marry Bruce, I was with him much longer than I should have been because I didn't have the time or energy to break it off. He'd randomly show up at places I was, and I'd smile and be polite, but towards the end, there was no sense of urgency to go out on dates.

Then of course he hated Ford, and the time I spent with Ford and Izzy. Ford didn't like him much which is my world is a huge red flag. Anytime, I'd pick Ford and Izzy 100% over anyone else. I think I just didn't want to deal with the fight I knew ending things would cause.

Shortly after the breakup, he left for Helena for some big, fabulous job and that was that. I wouldn't have even thought to add him to the list of suspects, but if Ford thinks he should be on it then so be it.

"What about the other guys?" I ask, wanting to not talk about Bruce anymore.

"Jackson is looking into the new guy. He found out his name is Ace, but we haven't been able to talk to him just yet. Miles will be at the school tomorrow since Fridays are when he normally comes to talk to you and we know he will be there. Asher is going to talk to Ruby to see if there is anyone else we need to add to the list."

"Well, hopefully we can wrap this up fast. I don't like all the not knowing," I sigh and finish off the rest of my wine.

Ford takes the glass from me and places it in the kitchen sink but then turns to look at me.

"Until we do figure it out, I think you should stay here," he says. By the look on his face I can tell he's serious.

"Well, I plan to stay for a few more days at least until the windows are fixed. Little too cold in the house otherwise. I mean, as long as it's okay that I stay here."

"Of course, you can stay here, but I mean even after

that you should stay here until we figure out who it is that broke into your house. Just in case they try to do it again."

"Why would they try to break into my house again? They got the only thing of value," I ask. But the cloud that crosses over his face tells me this isn't a conversation he wants to have.

"Ford?" I ask again when he doesn't answer my question.

"They may have taken the ring, but what if they were originally there to do harm to you?" He says his voice lacking emotion.

By the way he's clenching his jaw, I can tell just the thought upsets him. He's always been very protective of me.

"What if we never find out who did it at some point I have to go back to my own house I can't stay here forever," I protest trying to play devil's advocate.

"We will find out who did this and I will make sure that you are safe before you go back to your house. Just give me a little bit of time. Please."

As much as I'm protesting going back to my own house, I do want to stay here. I feel safe, knowing that somebody, some stranger was in my house going through my things really creeps me out.

Actually, I don't know how I'm going to be able to go back to that house because even after it's clean, that's all I'll see.

I'm going to have to buy new sheets, new underwear, and new towels. All the basics. I don't think I'm going to be able to use the old ones again. God only knows what the stranger did to them.

"I will stay here for now," I agree.

The look of pure relief on Ford's face does give me a bit of pause though.

CHAPTER 5
FORD

TODAY IS the Valentine's Day party at school and it's all Izzy has been talking about. She's been staying after school to help Luna with things. Then they bring home stuff to do and after dinner the three of us work on it. But today is the day I help out in the classroom.

Even though I love my girl to death, I was never a kid person. How Luna does it every day is beyond me, but I know how much this means to her and Izzy so I can do it for one day for them.

I'd do anything for them.

As the kids start piling into the classroom, they look at me and Izzy. Quickly, I make sure everyone knows I'm her dad. Though I do get a few looks from some of the kids' mothers which cause a few whispers, but otherwise it goes smoothly.

Luna goes through her morning routine with the kids. Then she introduces me and we get started on the crafts projects her and Izzy have been planning out all week.

My job is to go around, help any kid who needs it and to keep the mess

to a minimum. Luna kept stressing that the less mess there is the less time it will take us to clean up at the end of the day. But we had to allow enough of a mess so the kids would still enjoy themselves.

"Today is all about the kids having fun," she kept stressing on the way into school today.

Everything is Valentine's Day themed, from the book that she reads, to the snacks that Emma brought in, to the little goodie bags that she and Izzy put together for everyone.

I love watching her with all the kids. I've always known she's good with kids and everyone raves that she's such a great teacher, but I've never actually seen her in action like this.

She's so patient with the kids, and seems to understand what they're asking or saying even when they can't get the words out. I can't remember once having a teacher as attentive and involved as she is.

She doesn't get mad when one of the kids spills their juice, she just helps them clean up and move on. When another kid is tired and overstimulated, she lets them go hang out in a quiet corner for a little bit and doesn't even get upset when they doze off for a nap.

Izzy is right there to help her with anything she needs, but Luna does very good to make sure she's not playing favorites with her either. I'm very proud that

Izzy seems to understand this and doesn't get upset by it.

The day flies by so much faster than I expected. Before I knew it, kids are getting picked up by their parents. The same moms that were whispering about me this morning when they dropped their kids off are here, only this time their hair and makeup is done and they're dressed up as they try to grab my attention.

To make it clear that I'm not interested, I focus all my attention on Luna. As I help her clean up, I ignore the other woman. At the end of the day when all the other kids are gone and we're about to head out the door, in walks Ruby of all people.

"Oh, I'm glad I caught you both. I had gotten this gift card to the Flathead Steakhouse over there at the ski resort. Orville and I were going to go tonight to celebrate Valentine's Day, but he's got some emergency meeting and it has to be used with our reservation tonight. It's one of those discount one where we lose half the value if it's not used tonight. Anyway, I was thinking the two of you could use it." She says, pulling out the card and handing it to me.

"Ruby, this is really short notice and I can't take Izzy there," I shake my head.

That restaurant is very nice but they tend to frown on bringing kids. It's the kind where men have to wear a tie and women need a dress. No jeans or tennis shoes allowed. You get dirty looks if you leave your phone on the table. But the food is the best around, maybe the best in the whole state.

"Well, of course I thought of that. I will watch her. I'll be home alone anyway and could use the company. Besides," she steps closer to be and lowers her voice, "With everything Luna here has been through, it would be good to get her mind off it and get out of town for a bit."

She winks at me when she steps back, and I know I can't say no now. Ruby has this way of perfectly manipulating a situation, while covering all her bases before she even talks to you so you don't have a way to tell her no. That has worked out in the towns favor as a whole, but when she focuses on that on you, it's not a fun time.

"Izzy, how would you like to go have dinner with Ruby tonight?" I ask hoping my daughter will get me out of all this, but of course Izzy loves everyone and there is no such chance.

"Really?! Tonight? I can't wait! Will you paint my nails like you did last time?" she asks as she runs over to Ruby's side.

"Only if you do my toes like you did last time!" Ruby giggles like a schoolgirl as she leans in to hug Izzy.

"Well, that just leaves you and me," I say, looking up at Luna. "Would you like to have dinner with me tonight?"

"Umm, yes I would but," she trails off, looking down at her feet.

Instinctively I take a step toward her, wanting to make what the problem is right.

"Oh child. I stopped by your house. Miles and

Asher were there and I grabbed that blue dress you wore to the winter ball. It was still hanging in your closet, but I washed it anyway. It's in my car along with some shoes and jewelry for you to wear," Ruby smiles.

Luna's eyes light up when she says this and I know I'd stand in line for an hour at the worst restaurant in the world if that is what Luna wanted to do tonight.

"Let's head home and get ready then." I go to Luna's desk and pick up her bag she always brings home with her full of things to get ready for the next day.

With it being Friday, I assume she's going to be getting ready for next week.

"Okay," she says gently.

Why does this all the sudden feel so different? Like it's not just dinner with my best friend?

Dammit Ruby.

CHAPTER 6
LUNA

IT'S JUST dinner with Ford.

It's just Valentine's Day dinner with my best friend.

Something about tonight feels so much bigger than just dinner with Ford. I've never been this nervous with him before. Not on any first date, or even any dinner with Ford.

Maybe it's because it's a Valentine's Day dinner and something about it seems extra special. It's the day you have dinner with someone that you love, like a long-time partner or spouse. That has to be what my nerves are.

It's not because of the feelings I've been having living here with Ford. Between the break-in and everything going on, my emotions are all over the place. I think naturally I'm just looking to cling to someone and Ford happens to be the person that is right in front of me.

I've been having to remind myself of that more and more as I watch him with his daughter, especially when I watched him helping out at the Valentine's Day party today. Maybe it's just been too long since I've been laid is why I'm having some of these feelings.

I have to be projecting feelings onto Ford. Recently I've been thinking lots about starting my own family and that has to be what's causing all of this, I'm sure of it.

It makes me so happy Ruby was able to get my dress and have it cleaned for me because it is one of my favorites. Not to mention, it's also the most I've ever spent on a dress, and I will wear it as many times as I can to get my money's worth. The way it hugs my curves in all the right places and makes my breasts look amazing, and gives me such a boost of confidence.

As a girl with a little extra weight, anytime I can find something that makes me feel like a million bucks, well, I will wear the hell out of it.

Taking one last look in the mirror, I take a deep breath and push aside the feelings I've been having and go downstairs.

I find Ford in dress pants, a button-down shirt, and a tie. This man sure as hell knows how to clean up good. Ford may be my best friend, but I can still appreciate his looks and mountain man muscles that charm all the ladies who drool over him whether he realizes it or not.

"Wow, Luna you look... Wow," he says as his eyes run up and down my body and I can feel every inch that they examine. I can't recall a single time I've ever stunned a guy to almost silence, and it feels pretty damn good.

"You clean up pretty well yourself there," I tell him, earning me a slight smile.

Walking over to me, he picks up my jacket and helps me put it on before giving me his arm.

"Let's go and enjoy our dinner," he says, leading me out to his truck.

Opening the door, he helps me inside, and waits till I'm buckled up before closing the door and rounding the truck to his side. Once he's in, he turns the heat on and lets the truck warm up before we get on our way.

He keeps looking over at me and smiling, but the tension is thick in the air. I'm not sure what to do to break it and he doesn't seem to know either because we both sit there slightly awkwardly.

When we're underway, he messes with the heat before smiling again.

"Are you warm enough?" he asks.

"Yes, I promise I am plenty warm. Remember, I grew up here?" I tease him a little bit, and that seems to be enough to break the ice enough that we jump into our normal conversation for the rest of the drive.

When we get to the restaurant, we pull up and there's valet parking that is included because this place is just that expensive. I've been here only one other time in my life and that was for my high school graduation when my parents brought me up here because I graduated in the top ten of my class.

"Stay here and wait for me," he says gently before getting out of the truck.

He hands the keys to the valet, and they exchange a few words before the valet hands him his ticket. He then walks over to my door, opens it, offering me his hand as I step down.

Placing my hand in his, I'm getting ready to step out and the shocks that I feel where my skin touches him catch me completely off guard. I jerk my hand back and stare at his hand as if it had just bitten me. When I look up, he's staring down at his hand, dumbfounded as well, before his eyes gently meet mine.

Hesitantly, I place my hand in his again and this time he holds it firmly even with the sparks still there. When I step out of the warm truck into the cold Montana air, I don't feel any of it. The only thing I feel is the sparks between my hand and his.

He slowly helps me into the restaurant where we find that Ruby booked us one of the best tables in the house. Of course she did. The last time I was here, I remember thinking what a fairy tale like restaurant this was.

Everyone is dressed up in their best clothing, and the chances of seeing some fancy celebrity here I always thought were pretty high.

"Luna, look at me, ignore all of them. It's just you and me and some fancy clothes," Ford says pulling my attention away and essentially calming my nerves instantly.

He understands the feeling of not fitting in more

than anyone, and he's always been great at redirecting my mind when it goes there. I want to be able to do the same thing for him, so I know I need to give him my full attention.

"We should take bets on how many people will see propose while we're here," Ford says.

"It is Valentine's Day so that heavily increases the chances. I say no less than six," I challenge him.

He takes it seriously and looks around the room before answering me.

"I think we can get at least that possibly even ten," he says.

Almost as it was planned, the first of the proposal happens several tables away.

It's a little hard to hear what's being said, but when she says yes and nods her head, the whole restaurant cheers. There's a round of congratulations before everyone starts talking again.

"One down, five more to go," I laugh, shaking my head.

By the time our meals arrived, we saw a total of four proposals in the restaurant.

"You know Ruby will never let us live it down if we don't order dessert. Plus, it gives us the best chance of hitting our six proposals," he jokes.

But of course, we were going to order dessert, because it's my weakness and he knows it.

As we place our dessert order, we watch proposal number five happen. This one you can tell was a complete shock and for a heartbreaking moment, I almost thought she was going to say no but she doesn't. There was a collective sigh throughout the restaurant.

Before our check comes, Ford's phone rings. He looks at it and then looks at me.

"It's Ruby," he says answering it and I know we're both worried something's wrong.

After answering the phone, instantly his face relaxes..

"Yeah, that's fine." He pauses for a moment before he answers again. "Just have her call me in the morning."

When he gets off the phone, he chuckles.

"Ruby said that they were watching TV, and she fell asleep. Previously, she tried to wake Izzy up, but she was just so exhausted she insisted that we leave her there for the night and come get her in the morning, so I agreed," he says.

"You know Ruby will spoil her with pancakes and all the works before she even allows you to come to get her. Izzy will enjoy every minute of it." I tell him, trying to reassure him.

"I know. But I've spent very few nights away from her."

"Well then, I'm glad I'm here so that I can distract you," I say not really thinking. Yet when he looks at me again, the heat in his eyes is undeniable.

"I'm glad you're here for that and many other reasons," he says, and I honestly have no idea how to respond.

We finish our desserts, watching two more

proposals for a total of seven. Ford remains the perfect gentleman as he allows me to stand inside where it's nice and warm as he goes to get his truck. He then helps me in and makes sure I'm comfortable as we head back to his house.

The entire drive there we keep looking at each other and I wonder if he's thinking and feeling the same things as I am. Tonight, felt so much bigger, but it was different too.

Once we get to his place and we're inside where it's warm, he turns to me and it's almost like the awkward first date moves. Telling each other that we had a great time and the whole 'will he kiss me or won't he kiss me' thing runs through my mind. Only I don't really expect him to kiss me because this is Ford.

So, when he reaches forward and tucks a strand of hair behind my ear, I almost stopped breathing. His eyes met mine, and without thinking about it I licked my lips.

Then before I know it, his lips are on mine. Then he's backed me up to the wall, and those electric sparks singed me. Yeah, they are so much more intense now. I've never felt anything like it in my life.

They feel so good I can't stop the moan that is building and that's when Ford pulls away.

"Shit. Luna. I don't know... Fuck. I'm sorry," he says, running his hand through his hair.

"Why did you stop?" I asked without thinking, because that was the best damn kiss I'd ever had, and I certainly didn't want it to stop.

"Because it's us. I can't lose that." He shakes his head.

"I really liked that kiss," I tell him, biting my lip because I can still feel his lips on mine.

When he rubs his thumb over my bottom lips, it sends tingles straight to my core.

"I did too." He whispers resting his forehead against mine.

I knew tonight felt bigger, but I never thought he felt the same way I did.

"This isn't a one-time thing with us." He whispers, squeezing his eyes shut.

"No, I think this has been building," I agree. Then I wrap my arms around his neck.

"It definitely has on my end."

"Then what are we waiting for?" I make the move this time and lean, in bringing our lips together.

Now it's him who groans as he runs his hands along the side of my body, over my ass, and down the backs of my thighs before lifting me up and pulling my legs around his waist.

Feeling his hard, thick length against my core, makes my breasts ache in need. He carries me to his room, laying me on the bed where he deepens the kiss and runs his hands through my hair.

"The first time you wore this dress, it had me hard as nails, but even more so tonight." He admits, tracing the neckline down to the plunge between my breasts.

Reaching behind me, he unzips the dress before sliding it off my body, leaving me in nothing but my bra and underwear. When he stands to remove his clothes, I reach for the blanket to cover myself. I've always been a bigger girl and never comfortable in my own skin without clothes on.

"The fuck are you doing? I finally get you in my bed and you want to hide from me?" He asks, ripping the blanket away from me.

I'm stunned and don't even know what to say. When I open my mouth, nothing comes out. His face softens as he removes his shirt and pants before crawling back into bed with me.

"Every part of you is beautiful, Luna. Your curves are the sexiest thing I've ever seen. Both in and out of your clothes. Don't hide them from me." He says as he traces a finger over my stomach.

Though I try to believe him and relax, it doesn't come easy.

Then he removes my bra and settles in beside me, paying attention and slowly loving each of my breasts like they are the most delicate thing in the world. Maybe to him, they are.

Taking his time, he places kisses all over my body until I think I can't stand it anymore. Only then does he remove the rest of our clothes and reach into the night sand for a condom.

"All you have to say is stop," he looks at me hesitantly.

"I don't want to stop," I tell him shaking my head.

"Good, because I've never wanted anything so

damn bad in my life." He slides the condom on in no time and is back in bed with me.

The whole time I'm watching him, all his muscles are on full display. He has the hard-earned body any woman would love to look at. As he climbs on top of me, his muscles make me feel small. He cages me in and his face is close to mine.

Our eyes lock and I know I don't want to miss a moment of this, so I barely breathe as he starts to slide into me. I moan because nothing has ever felt so good.

"Fuck, I'm not going to last, you feel so damn good." He groans into my ear as he kisses my neck.

His lips sear my body, and I can feel every place his skin is touching mine.

"I don't know if I want to make you cum or if I want this moment to last all night."

"Cum now and go again later tonight," I tell him desperately with the need to finish and take him over the edge with me.

"I like how you think."

With one arm he pulls one of my legs up and the change of angle has each thrust giving delicious pressure to my clit. I'm digging my nails into his back, trying to hold myself together for something that is stronger, more wonderful than I've ever felt in my life.

"Come for me, beautiful. I can't wait to feel you squeezing me and watch you come undone for me." When he bites my bottom lip, it throws me over the edge.

I scream his name, enjoying that I've set him off

too. Getting to share this moment together means I'll never forget it.

Once we catch our breath, he collapses on top of me.

"I'll move in a minute, I just need to regain some strength. Yeah, I'm pretty sure your pussy tried to suck out my soul," he says.

"Well, I don't think I can move after that," I hum.

"Let me get cleaned up. I'm going to hold you while I regain some energy for round two," he says.

There are many things you shouldn't know about your best friend, like what it feels like to have their dick inside of you, what it's like to kiss them or what they look like naked.

So adding cuddling to that list doesn't seem like such a big deal.

CHAPTER 7
FORD

FUCK, my head is so messed up right now.

Last night was by far the most amazing night of my entire life. Luna is everything I've ever wanted, but she's my best friend and last night should not have happened. Then again, last night there was no stopping me even if I had tried. Lord knows I sure as hell did not even try.

At one point after I had had her several times, she got up, putting on my shirt to use the bathroom. The sight of her in nothing but my shirt is something I know I will never forget.

Currently, I'm downstairs making breakfast. When I got up, she was still fast asleep in my shirt, and I didn't have the heart to wake her. But damn, did she look good in my bed.

I'm so lost in my thoughts picturing her still in my bed that I don't hear her enter the room until she says good morning.

"Hey, breakfast is almost ready," I tell her, not sure what else to say.

"So, I was thinking and last night was amazing, but I know you said you would never commit to someone again and I really don't want to ruin our friendship. It's best we leave this as a great night together, but nothing more." She smiles, turning to make her coffee.

"Sounds good to me," I tell her, even though the words sound bitter in my mouth.

Even though I have said that I won't commit to someone again multiple times, for some reason when thinking about Luna that thought never crossed my mind. I'm already committed to her in a different way.

After finishing up breakfast, I set it down in front of her just as my phone went off.

> Jackson: Everyone to Luna's in an hour. I found something.

"Eat up. It looks like it's going to be a busy morning. Would you mind going and picking up Izzy from Ruby's and bringing her back here? I'm meeting the guys at your house it looks like they might have found something?" I'm happy about the change in subject.

"Of course. Did they say what they found?" she asks, looking a little nervous.

"No, but hopefully it's a good lead."

After breakfast, we get ready and do not mention what happened last night. When I step out of the bathroom after getting ready, I stare at the bed. The sheets are still rumpled and you can clearly see where Luna had been laying last night. I'm willing to bet if I lean down, it will even smell like her. Shaking my head, I turn and walk out of my room. Right now, I can't go down that road.

"I'm heading out to get Izzy. Is there anything she needs to do when we get back?" Luna asks, not looking at me. I hate not having her eyes on me.

"Make sure she takes a shower, puts on some clean clothes, and brushes her hair and teeth really well. Lord only knows what happened at Ruby's last night."

"Sounds good. Be safe and let me know if you hear anything."

Walking out together, it's like I've always done it. When we get to her car, I open the door and wait for her to get settled.

At some point in high school, I made it up in my head that I was going to show her how she should be treated so that maybe she wouldn't settle for less. Now it's just a habit, one that after last night I sure as hell don't want to break.

Then I follow her down the mountain to make sure she gets into town okay, and then we go our separate ways.

As I'm driving to her house, I debated if I tell the guys what happened. After thinking for a moment, I decide to keep it to myself. At least for now.

When I get there Miles and Asher are already there. They're sitting on the porch talking, so I get out and join them.

"We heard Ruby corralled you and Luna to dinner last night. How did that go?" Miles jokes.

"How the hell did you hear about it so fast?" I grumble. Not liking how easily my business is traveling, even in a town as small as Mustang Mountain.

"My sister may be new here, but she is plenty connected in the gossip tree. Don't even ask me how. It's just a gift she has I think." Miles shakes his head.

"Well, if she could use that gift to figure out who did this, that would be great." I wave my hand at the house just as Jackson pulls up, with another truck right behind him that I don't recognize.

"Guys, this is Ace," Jackson says introducing us to the man walking up with him. "He's new in town. Ex-military with some excellent tracking skills. When I told him what was going on, he offered to come and take a look at the place to see if we missed anything. I figured an extra set of eyes couldn't hurt." Jackson looks at me with a nod. I'll take any extra eyes that I can to help Luna out.

This also means it rules out him as a suspect. I'm not sure if I'm happy or disappointed about that. Glad to rule out someone who's willing to help, I guess, but also disappointed that we still don't have any leads.

Jackson explains the details that we know and how we found the house. Following Ace in, I give him space to do whatever he is he's going to do. He's very thorough and looks over each room in the house, asking questions like where the ring was stored, who knew about it, and things like that. Then he goes out the back porch, looking around and we follow him through the backyard.

"There's a trail heading through these trees and it's freshly upturned. Have you followed this?" he asks once we reach the tree line in her backyard.

"No, and Luna won't be out in the woods, especially not by herself in the winter," I tell him and he nods. We quietly follow him through the woods, making as little noise as possible, completely unsure of what we might find.

Part of me wonders if this is just wasting time. For all you know, this is the path that Hades took when he came into the house and laid on the front porch that night. But the logical side of my brain says there are no paw prints, so it wasn't Hades that made this trail.

The trail leads right into the backyard of another house that is the next street over.

"This place has been abandoned for a few years," Asher says what we are all probably thinking.

Stopping at the tree line, I looked over at Ace and Jackson.

"Asher and Miles you two go around to the front, the three of us will come up the back," Jackson whispers. We give them a head start so they can go the long way.

Once we saw them cross over to the front, we head towards the back of the house. Since the back door lock is busted, we quietly open it, only to find the house inside completely trashed.

This means someone's been living here because the

family that moved out cleaned the place and left it in good condition, I was on the crew who helped them move out. It's was nothing like what we see before us. There are food wrappers scattered everywhere and dirty clothes in the corner.

I would almost think the place has been used for some teens to have a party, but there are no beer cans or alcohol bottles scattered anywhere. Silently, we make our way around to the living room where the other guys are. It looks like none of us found anything.

About to speak when suddenly we hear footsteps, yet all five of us are standing still. Turning in the direction of the hallway where they're coming from, no other than Luna's ex-boyfriend Bruce steps out into the room. He has a baseball bat, but that won't make any difference because all of us are carrying guns.

Ace is the only one to pull his gun, while Jackson and I approach him on either side ready to disarm him.

"Was it you that broke into Luna's house?" I ask.

"That bitch owed me, so I took payment," he shrugs, as if it's no big deal that he just admitted to a crime.

"What did she owe you?" Miles asks.

"She ruined my reputation here and made it impossible for me to get a job. Then I had to move out of town. Even then she still managed to trash my name." He sneers and focuses on Jackson, which allows me to take another step toward him.

This man is absolutely delusional. Luna has never held a grudge against anyone in her life. But judging by the marks on his arm and the wild look in his eyes, I can pretty much guarantee I know why his name was trashed.

"Are you sure it was Luna and not your drug habit?" I ask, pulling his attention to me, allowing Jackson to advance on him.

"I've got that under control, the only way someone would know about it is if they were told about it. Apparently, just like Luna told you." He laughs, but it's more of a manic laugh than someone who finds something truly entertaining.

"Luna didn't tell me about the marks all over your arm and the look in your eye. If someone knows what to look for, it's very obvious in you." I tell him, keeping his attention on me.

"Well, of course it's gotten worse since I've been out of work, lost my house, and no one's willing to help me." He rolls his eyes and his eyes swings over to Jackson.

He points the bat at Jackson almost like he's saying don't take another step.

"So that's why you broke into Luna's house and stole her grandmother's ring?" I ask, trying to get him to refocus.

"The bitch was always talking about how valuable it was and that was the only thing of value that she had. It's like she was asking for it to be taken," he says when he finally looks back over at me.

"Or maybe she was sharing something important with someone who she thought cared about her," Miles says from the other side of me, allowing Jackson to advance and knock him to the ground.

Bruce is definitely on something. Jackson's a big guy, but Bruce is able to toss him off of him like he weighs nothing. So Miles and I jumped in. Between the three of us, we're able to pin him down. Jackson steps outside to call his cop friend and Ace joins us, pulling some zip ties from his pocket to help detain Bruce.

"Where is the ring?" I ask. I'm hoping I can figure out where it is and get it back for her.

"As I've told you, she doesn't deserve that damn ring," he says. Unfortunately, my boot makes contact with his ribs, making him grunt.

After that, he refuses to talk. The police get there pretty quickly, and we explain what happened. Thankfully, Bruce is pretty vocal by then and in front of the police again admits to what he did all on the basis that Luna deserved it.

That woman is the most remarkable person I've ever met, and she doesn't deserve anything close to what this horrible person did to her.

On the way back over to get our trucks, a thought pops into my head.

"I bet he pawned the ring at a pawn shop," I say.

"Yes, but it wouldn't have been a local one, because anyone here would have recognized the ring. He would have had to go somewhere where he would not be recognized."

After dividing up the local shops that surround

Mustang Mountain, we each decided to make some phone calls and see if we could find the ring.

Bruce may be going to jail for a really long time, but that's not quite enough for me. I need to make sure she gets back that ring.

I'll do anything to make it happen.

CHAPTER 8
LUNA

TO SAY it's been a huge relief to know that the person that broke into my house is behind bars, but it still shakes me up to know it was my ex. At one point, I thought he was a good person, that he was someone I could see a life with really upsets me.

Ford told me that Bruce is on drugs and I know that it can change someone, but to know that my gut was so far off about him really disturbs me.

Even though I take comfort in Ford's words, I keep attempting to figure out what red flags I missed. Were there signs I ignored that I shouldn't have? I don't want to make the same mistake again, but to do that I have to know what I missed. Especially now, being back at work isn't the time to think about it.

The kids make me smile and get my mind off of Bruce. Usually, if they can tell that I'm even slightly upset, every one of them wants to come and give me a hug and cheer me up.

Today I was more successful in hiding my swirling thoughts than yesterday. When Izzy decided to have lunch with one of her friends instead of wanting to stay in the classroom and eat with me, I got a little time to myself to decompress and regroup, which I think was a huge help.

While I love Izzy to death, she will talk on and on about something for an hour straight and then switch topics so fast it'll give you whiplash. If I had even half of that girl's energy, I would be a much different person..

After all the kids have left, I'm finishing packing up my room for the day when Ford walks in. Izzy ran right up to him and gave him a hug, which warmed my heart. I love watching these two interact both here at school and at home. He gives her a hug before turning to look at me.

"Can we talk for a moment?"

I can tell by his tone that it's something serious.

"Yeah, just let me ask another teacher to watch Izzy real quick," I say, wanting to make sure she is out of earshot for whatever he has to say because I can tell it's serious.

She follows me across the hall where she's more than excited to play with a whole new set of toys that I don't have in my classroom. After she grabs some blocks, she doesn't even notice when I leave the room.

"Everything okay?" I ask, walking back into my classroom and finding Ford leaning against my desk with his arms folded across his chest.

"So, the guys and I just finished up at your house. Everything's been picked up and cleaned, and the windows and doors fixed. While we were there, were able to wash and dry a few loads of laundry, but pretty much everything else has to be washed, and you're going to have to get almost all new food."

"So it's safe for me to go back?"

"Yes, eventually."

"What do you mean eventually?" I ask him confused.

I'm more than ready to get back into my own space, and to be back into my own home. After our night together, I need some space and distance between him and me.

It's exhausting trying to keep up a front, especially around his daughter. I don't ever want her to think there is something wrong with us. She would keep prying until she figured it out and I don't want her to think about the possibility of her dad and me getting together.

Izzy has asked me more than once if I'd be her mommy. She wanted to know why can't I marry her dad and be her mom. There were other variations along the same lines. I don't want to give her hope when there isn't.

"I mean, I don't think it's time for you to move back in yet," he says, shocking me.

"Why not? We caught who did it and the house is secured again."

I always thought once we knew who did it and the

house was fixed, I would be moving back in. But there is some reason Ford seems hesitant about me moving back and I would like to understand why.

Seemingly irritated, he stands and paces around the room. "Bruce may be in custody, but he hasn't been charged. He could still make bail, get released, and then you would be home alone."

"So you want me to stay with you until he's been sentenced?" I asked confused.

"It would be safest, so yes," he says without missing a beat.

This has to be a joke. I start laughing and shaking my head.

"Ford, that could be months. I'm not sitting around for months on end. In the meantime, I'll arm and protect myself, but I'm not going to sit scared." Putting my foot down on the matter, I cross my arms.

How could he not see how easy it would be to ruin our friendship the longer I stay? What he doesn't know is that night was more than just a one-time thing for me. It was the best night of my life, and it hurts so much to know that it will never be anything more. It's painful thinking that I will be nothing more than a one-night stand with my best friend.

Seeing him every day and remembering what it's like to wake up in bed is just too much. Needing to get out of there, I know now is a perfect time so I don't understand this hesitation.

"At least wait until this weekend so the guys and I can help you." He tries one more time.

"Help me with what? I brought one suitcase over that will fit in my car and I can stop at the Mercantile and get some food. There's no reason to prolong this."

"Damn it, Luna. Why do you have to be so stubborn," he says, clenching and unclenching his fists.

"You knew this about me from day one. I've always been stubborn, and I've always done things my own way. That doesn't end now." I tell him, packing up the rest of the stuff I will be taking with me for the night.

I do still have to ride home with him and Izzy, but I know that Izzy will distract us by sharing everything that happened today.

While I can tell he's not happy with me, I know I can't live the rest of my life in fear, either. Pasting on a big smile, I grab my stuff and head over to get Izzy from the other classroom. She's so full of energy and joy that she doesn't pick up that her father is irritated.

"So, what did you do today?" he asks. This question will ensure that she will not stop talking the entire way home.

Izzy tells us about her day, including a full play-by-play of what happened at recess with one of her friends.

When he keeps looking over at me, I offer him a small smile in hopes of not drawing attention from Izzy. She finally stops talking when we're just a few minutes from the cabin, so I chime in.

"Your dad and his friends have been working really hard to get my house ready for me. So, I'm going to be packing up and heading home tonight."

"But it's mac and cheese night! We're supposed to make mac and cheese tonight, *not* the kind from the box. Can't you at least stay through the weekend?" she whines.

I look over at Ford and his eyes are wide.

"You coached her to say that, didn't you?"

"I swear to you I did not. Maybe you should listen because it's good advice," he says with a little laugh.

"No, I just want to sleep in my own bed. The longer I wait, the more I'm going to build this up in my head." I try to be truthful.

"Well, you're brave. If my house was broken in, I don't think I'd be able to sleep in there again," Izzy says while shaking her head in all seriousness.

It's nice to know a 5-year-old thinks I'm brave because I sure as hell don't feel like it right now.

CHAPTER 9
FORD

NOW THAT LUNA IS GONE, I'm really starting to notice it. She just fit into our life here. Making dinner without her felt wrong.

In no time, she was packed up and ready to go. It was almost like she was running from something. But I get what she isn't saying. She needs space from me and from us. Though I don't think space is a good thing.

If I know her, she will just get in her head and overthink it all. So much so it could ruin us. That night we shared was magical, and I'd absolutely do it again. She is the one who put up the roadblocks and I let her. While I respect them, I don't want her turning it into something it wasn't. I can't stop her from thinking if she isn't here.

Making dinner tonight had a sad tone to it, and even Izzy picked up on it. It's hitting even more now as I try to put Izzy to bed. She had gotten used to Luna helping me at bedtime. We'd also read the book together doing the voices. Izzy loved it and it always had Luna laughing, which made me smile. It was an all-around good way to end the day.

"I love you Daddy, but you're not as good with the voices as Luna is. Maybe tomorrow night we can call her and have her read them on the phone," Izzy says with all seriousness.

"I don't know, baby. It's going to take Luna a bit to get used to being home again. She has to get back into her own routines."

"Then can we ask her to help read the book?" Izzy asks again.

"Once she is settled, we can ask." I give in because I don't want her to think there is any other reason to not ask.

I read her an extra book to make up for it, even though I know it was not my fault. Once she's finally asleep, I head back downstairs, clean up and get ready for the next day.

Luna and I had a great routine down. I made lunch for her and Izzy and got the coffee ready, while she cleaned up the kitchen. Then I took care of the trash and started some laundry. Now I do it all myself thinking of Luna the whole time until my phone goes off.

> Lura: I made it safe. Grabbed food at the Mercantile too.

Well, at least she is still acting normal, letting me know she got in safe.

> Me: Good. Lock up the house.
>
> Luna: I will. Hades looks like he's camping out on the porch, so I'm going to feed him first.

I need to find a way to spoil the heck out of that wolf. Since this all happened, he has been great at protecting Luna and her house.

> Me: Good, that makes me feel better that he's there watching out for you.
>
> Luna: Me too.
>
> Me: The house isn't the same without you.
>
> Luna: I miss our reading time with Izzy.
>
> Me: She was asking about you reading to her again. I said we'd ask once you were settled again.
>
> Luna: I'm going to get ready for bed. Thank you for everything.
>
> Me: Anything for you.

I should be going to bed as well. As I make one last loop around the house, I know I'm just stalling.

Finally, I go upstairs and stop in my doorway. Just looking at my bed, I see her there. The last few nights I've fallen asleep in my chair next to the bed because I haven't wanted to mess up the area she had been in.

Tonight I lie down on the side of the bed where I

slept and turn to face the side she was on. I can still smell her there. Right now, right here, I want nothing more than to cuddle with her again. I had no intention of putting a stop to any of this, but she is right about what I said.

I just don't know how to tell her I want more, that I didn't want to stop. She was so relieved when I told her that the person who broke into her house was behind bars that she gave me a happy hug. Even in front of Izzy, it still felt good to have her in my arms.

While I tried to prolong getting her house ready, part of me knew as soon as it was ready she would want to move back into it and I can't blame her. If the situation was reversed, I'd want to be back in my own space as soon as possible too. But I was really hoping for more time, even just through the weekend, so I could better prepare myself for her leaving.

At some point, I fall asleep and dream of her back in my arms. But waking up with her scent surrounding me from the pillow she used is a real mindfuck.

As I work on getting Izzy ready for school, I see Luna in every space of my house. She's enjoying her morning coffee at the dining room table, she's making us pancakes at the stove, cleaning dishes at the sink, reading to Izzy on the couch, and walking through the front door after forgetting her phone in the car.

"Are you okay Daddy?" Izzy asks on the way to school.

"I'm fine peanut. Why?"

"Because you just passed the street that we turned

down to go to school, and I'm pretty sure you haven't listened to a word I said the entire way here," she sighs.

"Shit," I say pulling into an abandoned parking lot to make a U-turn.

"Now I know something's wrong because you never cuss unless you're stressed out," she says with a little sass from the back seat.

"Just a lot on my mind is all," I say.

"I don't cuss when I have a lot on my mind, Daddy."

When I see my opening to distract her, I take it.

"You are five. What could you possibly have on your mind?" I ask faking complete shock.

"Oh Daddy, you have no idea," she says, crossing her arms and getting ready to launch into a story just like I had hoped. "There's who I'm going to sit with at lunch today, who I'm going to play with on the playground, and what if Susie is still mad at Taylor? Then I can't sit with either of them at lunch, which means I have to sit with Ashley. The problem is Ashley's mom packs her smelly lunches, so I really don't want to sit there."

Until we get to the school, she goes on and on about playground drama. Even though I know Luna was probably in her classroom getting ready for the day, I scan the crowd for any glimpse of her I could possibly see.

"Have a good day at school, peanut," I tell her and kiss her before she jumps out of the car.

Then I go home to get some work done, but I can't seem to concentrate on anything. This house is one big reminder of Luna. Deciding to leave early, I head down to the mercantile and get some shopping done before I pick up Izzy.

When I step into the mercantile with the intention of grabbing a cup of coffee first, of course, it's Ruby that's behind the counter.

"You're a real idiot for letting Luna move back home," she tells me as she sets the coffee cup down in front of me.

"I tried to stop her and wanted her to wait until this weekend. Hell I wanted her to wait until Bruce was sentenced and there was no chance of him getting out on parole."

"None of that would have kept her there and you know it. You're telling me the whole time that she was living there nothing happened between the two of you? Nothing that you brushed off and made her think was unimportant? Nothing happened that you made her think you didn't want her?" Ruby says, pouring coffee into the cup.

Ruby has always been the matchmaker around town, and she has this sixth sense when it comes to couples. So it doesn't surprise me that she's seen right through me. Well, either that or it was an incredibly lucky guess.

No matter how she knows, the fact is, she's right. Getting Luna to stay was never about her safety in the house or when she should move back. It was wanting time with her and trying to find a way to tell her that I didn't want to stop. Even more, that I didn't want her in my bed to be a one-time thing.

When the hell did I fall in love with my best friend?

As that question floats through my mind, my knees almost buckle, and I have to grip the counter for support. If she doesn't feel the same way, I am so screwed. I also know I can't do this half-assed either. It's all or nothing.

"Will you pick Izzy up from school today?" I ask Ruby.

"Of course. She can help out around here. Do you have a plan?" Ruby asks with a huge smile on her face.

"I'm working on it." I put the money on the counter for the coffee and head right back to my truck.

If I want my plan to work, I've got to get a move on.

CHAPTER 10
LUNA

IT'S Saturday and my first full day off from school since moving back to my house. My home used to be my sanctuary, my place where I would go relax and unwind after a busy day. I looked forward to my nights alone here.

Now I dread every moment of being alone in this house.

I'm trying everything I can to keep myself busy. Instead of only working on the upcoming week, I have taken on extra work. Trying to get myself ahead for weeks in order to keep my mind occupied. I've even taken to teaching myself to knit by watching some online videos, but that doesn't even help.

My only comfort has been Hades who seems to realize that I need him. He's never been far, just like now he's lying on my back porch. Every night since I came back, he's been there and listened while I poured my heart out about how scared I was to be here. One night, I swear he was trying to tell me not to be scared because he had my back and wasn't going to let anything happen to me.

I'm sure it helps that I also spoiled the hell out of him with dinner each night. Not a bad gig, he sleeps on my porch with the blankets I provided, he gets a home-cooked meal each night, and have the days to run out and do as he pleases.

Though I wasn't so sure he was going to stick around today, but after breakfast, he hadn't left so I decided to make lunch and go sit on the porch with him.

Hades takes notice when I start cooking up the bacon for the BLT I'm making and searing up two burgers for him. When I fix us both a plate, pour him a bowl of water and myself a glass of soda, I place it all on a tray, grab an extra blanket, and head out to my back porch.

I turn on the heater because I love sitting outside to do school work or read and this makes it easier to do here in Montana.

"Alright, Hades, I really appreciate you hanging out with me today. So I made us lunch." At my words, he gets up, sits down next to my chair and just watches me. I place one of the burgers on a plate and set it on the ground for him along with his water, and he waits until I take the first bite of my sandwich before he leans in to eat his.

"Such good table manners. Can I tell you something?" I ask.

He looks up at me and tilts his head to the side as if I know what I'm talking about. I take it as a yes and continue.

"I think I really messed things up with Ford. We slept together one night, and it was amazing, like mind-blowing. I got scared because he's a no-commitment kind of guy and gave him an easy out. Only he wasn't pushing me away, and he didn't want me to move out of his place."

Stopping, I eat another bite of my lunch.

"I've been trying to call him and get nothing. No matter what time it is when I called, he used to always pick up. I've sent some texts, and he doesn't answer them until that night like before bed. It's as if I'm an afterthought."

After finishing the first burger, he looks up at me like he's trying to convey a message. While I'd like to think he wants to give me advice, in reality, he probably just wants his other burger. Which I give him and he starts chowing down on it.

"I should be more like you. A lone wolf, enjoying being on my own. No one to answer or worry about. I bet you are enjoying the single life, huh?"

As I'm finishing up lunch, sitting there petting him and thinking, I don't hear anyone approach, but Hades sure does. He stands and looks at my side gate but doesn't growl.

A moment later, Ford and Izzy round the corner and they are both dressed nicely like they just came from church.

Hades greeted them and let Izzy pet him before running off and disappearing into the woods behind my house.

As the climb the steps to the porch, Ford says.

"The house feels wrong without you there. I keep thinking you will walk through the door or around the corner and when you don't, my heart sinks."

"I miss you and Dad reading to me at night. He just can't do the voices like you can," Izzy says.

I laugh because I know Ford's princess voice and it's not very good.

"For one thing, I wasn't great at voicing why I didn't want you to leave the other day. Mostly because I couldn't say it myself. But it took Ruby, of all people, to put my feelings into words. Then it took me a few days to figure things out and talk to Izzy, but she's on board."

Why is Ruby always the voice of reason?

"Izzy and I talked and decided we have been ignoring things for a while," Ford says.

"And we want to go big!" Izzy says with a huge smile on her face.

"Okay?" I ask hesitantly, still not sure where this is going.

Ford reaches into his pocket and pulls something out before walking over to me and taking my hand in his free one.

"When we were younger, I knew you would be in my life forever, I just didn't know how. So I settled on you as my best friend. But I know now I want more," he says. Then he squeezes my hand, drops down to one knee and holds up a ring.

It took me a minute to realize it was my grandma's ring, the one that Brice stole and we never got back.

"Where did you get that?" I ask, not even bothering to stop the tears.

"The guys and I started calling pawn shops, and we got a few leads, so I visited each one myself. It took me the last few days, but I found it yesterday and was able to get it back for you. If I was going to ask you to marry me, I knew I was going to need this ring to do it."

He went to each pawn shop. Is that why he hasn't been reachable? Driving to some of the local towns means you are without reception or you are in and out of the calling area for an hour or more. Is that why he didn't text me until after nine at night when most of them closed?

Wait.

Did he just ask me to marry him?

"Marry you?" I ask in complete shock.

"Yes. I want to marry you. I want to spend the rest of my life with you, my best friend. I want you to move in with me and let me hold you each night, be part of my every day, help me read princess stories to Izzy and let me pick both of you up from school to go get pizza or ice cream. Even though I can't pinpoint the moment I fell in love with you, yet I am. Head over heels in love with you. Will you marry me?"

Behind him Izzy is about to burst with excitement. She has a huge smile on her face and is trying so hard not to jump up and down. She is nodding her head like crazy as if saying, please say yes.

Looking back at Ford, he's there with so much hope in his eyes. This is what I wanted, isn't it? This is what felt so right, and why it felt so wrong to walk away.

"Yes," I whisper so quietly I barely hear it. Not sure how they manage it, but I look down to see Ford placing the ring on my finger. Izzy screams and Ford stands and kisses me.

Even though it's a short kiss, it's intense. Since we are both aware we have little eyes watching.

"We will celebrate tonight. With you back in my bed." He whispers in my ear.

"Why don't we go mark this occasion with some ice cream in town? Then we can help her pack up some stuff and move back to the cabin tonight," Ford says to Izzy.

"Whoa, you want me to move back in with you tonight?" I asked dumbfounded.

"Yes. I don't want to wait to have you back with us. If you try and pull this not until we're married bullshit, I will march you down to the courthouse tonight and have a ring on your finger by Monday." The look he gives me lets me know he isn't joking.

"No, it's not that isn't just... I just got back here." I say looking at my house.

"Can you honestly tell me that you want to be here all by yourself?"

"Well... no but..."

"Then why put this off?"

"Is this how it's always going to be? You just kind of bulldoze the decision making?" I ask, but can't help smiling.

"On the important things that matter absolutely. How do you reckon I can make sure that you're safe, where I can hold you in my arms every night, or I can spend my time making you happy? That's absolutely the most important thing."

"Well, when you put it that way, how can I say no?" I sigh, acting like I'm frustrated, but he knows I'm not.

"You can't. That's the whole point." Izzy says, smiling as she skips in front of us on her way to the truck.

When he opens the door for Izzy, I reach for the door handle, and he stops me.

"Wait, that's my job. When she's in, I'll help you," he says, giving me a look like I should know this by now. It's nice to know that while our relationship might be changing, the important things between us are staying the same.

We head downtown to the ice cream shop where I see a few of my students and their families and I'm glad we're not the only people grabbing ice cream in February in Montana.

Izzy takes her time and looks at every flavor as if she hasn't visited this ice cream shop several times a month since the day she was born.

"Can we go eat these on the bench on the other side of the Mercantile?" Izzy asks once we all have our ice cream.

"You sure you're not going to be too cold for that?" Ford asks.

"Nope. When we're done, we can go warm up in the Mercantile and say hi to Ruby and tell her the good news."

With that, he leads us out of the ice cream shop onto the sidewalk. We don't even get to the corner before Izzy stops and points at a truck driving by.

"Isn't that Mile's truck?" she asks.

Sure enough, it drives by. Only he isn't alone. There is a woman in the front seat and normally this wouldn't be a big deal. But this isn't any woman, she's a bride in a full on wedding dress, hair and makeup done and the veil in place.

"What in the hell is going on?" Ford says under his breath as we both watch him drive down Main Street.

EPILOGUE
MILES

DRIVING through the middle of downtown Mustang Mountain wasn't how I liked to spend my Friday nights. But Jackson and Emma had invited me out to dinner to celebrate their engagement, so I'd gotten cleaned up and was on my way to the steakhouse. I hadn't quite forgiven him for taking up with my little sister, but a man could only hold a grudge for so long. It was time to make up, and I couldn't think of a better way to do it than over elk medallions and a stiff pour of bourbon. All on Jackson's dime, of course.

I was just about to the corner where the ice cream shop sat. Seemed pretty crowded for such a cold night. Back where I grew up in San Diego, when temps dipped into the sixties, people put on parkas and went out for hot chocolate. They never would have thought about eating ice cream. I chuckled to myself. That was one of the things I loved about living in Montana. The folks around Mustang Mountain never let the cold prevent them from doing anything.

I squinted as a family stepped out of the shop. Even from twenty yards away, I recognized Ford. He had one hand wrapped around a waffle cone, and the other behind the woman at his side. Thank fuck he'd come to his senses and got his head out of his ass when it came to Luna. The whole town could tell the two of them belonged together. Poor fucker was the last one to realize it.

Based on the lack of space between them, his efforts had paid off. It had taken the better part of a week to figure out who the fuck had gone after Luna, then a few more days for him to find that ring her douchebag ex had stolen and pawned.

My pulse spiked just thinking about it. With that dick behind bars, Ford would never have to worry about Luna's safety again.

I wondered if he'd popped the question yet. It was inevitable. First, Jackson and Emma. Now, Ford and Luna. Ruby's plan to get the Mustang Mountain Riders matched up might not be going exactly like she imagined, but love was in the air. I just hoped she didn't have any intention of making me part of her bullshit plan.

My life was perfect exactly like it was. I ran a successful software business that let me set my own hours, pick my own clients, and work from wherever I wanted. I'd built my cabin on Mustang Mountain with my own hands and didn't have to answer to anyone about anything. Yeah, I loved my life. Though, sometimes I wondered what it would be like to have someone to share it with. The light changed to green. Enough with the sappy introspection. I lifted my foot from the brake pedal and was about to step on the gas when a flurry of white appeared in my peripheral vision.

The passenger-side door opened and a huge white ball of lace jumped into the cab. "Go, go, go!"

"What the hell do you think you're doing?" I tightened my grip on the steering wheel. There was no reason for me to feel threatened by the woman underneath the layers and layers of white, but shit like this didn't happen in Mustang Mountain.

A face appeared in the middle of the big white bundle. Her cheek sported an angry red mark and appeared to be swelling by the second. Big brown eyes pleaded with me. "I've got to get out of here. Please."

I'd never seen her before in my life, but the fear in her eyes made a permanent imprint on me, and I knew as long as I lived, I'd never forget it. She looked like a wild animal who'd been fighting for its life, but now knew the end was near. The need to protect her surged within me. My foot hit the gas just as a dark-haired guy in a tux reached for the door handle.

The woman yelled as I accelerated. She grabbed onto my arm, her chest heaving hard underneath the layers and layers of shiny white fabric. I took the road out of town to put some distance between the two of us and whoever was after her. When we'd gone far enough, I pulled over to the side of the road.

I glanced over at her. Black lines streaked her cheeks. Her hair had come loose, and soft waves framed her face. She met my gaze for the briefest moment, her brown eyes full of apprehension. Fuck, she was beautiful. I felt the cage I'd built around my heart rattle.

Keeping my tone low and soft, I turned toward her and said, "I need to ask you something."

"What's that?" Her voice came out shaky and on the verge of tears.

"Who the hell are you?"

Make sure to grab your bonus scene of Ford and Luna for free!

Don't miss Mile's story in March is for Miles and get Asher's story in April is for Asher!

Or read where it all began with January is for Jackson!

MOUNTAIN MEN OF MUSTANG MOUNTAIN

Welcome to Mustang Mountain where love runs as wild as the free-spirited horses who roam the hillsides. Framed by rivers, lakes, and breathtaking mountains, it's also the place the Mountain Men of Mustang Mountain call home. They might be rugged and reclusive, but they'll risk their hearts for the curvy girls they love.

To learn more about the Mountain Men of Mustang Mountain, visit our website (https://www.matchofthemonthbooks.com/) join our newsletter here (http://subscribepage.io/MatchOfTheMonth) or follow our Patreon here (https://www.patreon.com/MatchOfTheMonth)

January is for Jackson - https://www.matchofthemonthbooks.com/January-Jackson

February is for Ford - https://www.matchofthemonthbooks.com/February-Ford

March is for Miles - https://www.matchofthemonthbooks.com/March-Miles

April is for Asher - https://www.matchofthemonthbooks.com/April-Asher

ACKNOWLEDGMENTS

A huge, heartfelt thanks goes to everyone who's supported us in our writing, especially our HUSSIES of Mountain Men of Mustang Mountain patrons:

Jackie Ziegler

To learn more about the Mountain Men of Mustang Mountain on Patreon, visit us here: https://www.patreon.com/MatchOfTheMonth

OTHER BOOKS BY KACI ROSE

Oakside Military Heroes Series
Saving Noah – Lexi and Noah
Saving Easton – Easton and Paisley
Saving Teddy – Teddy and Mia
Saving Levi – Levi and Mandy
Saving Gavin – Gavin and Lauren
Saving Logan – Logan and Faith
Saving Ethan – Bri and Ethan

Mountain Men of Whiskey River
Take Me To The River – Axel and Emelie
Take Me To The Cabin – Pheonix and Jenna
Take Me To The Lake – Cash and Hope
Taken by The Mountain Man - Cole and Jana
Take Me To The Mountain – Bennett and Willow
Take Me To The Edge – Storm

Mountain Men of Mustang Mountain
February is for Ford – Ford and Luna
April is for Asher – Asher and Jenna

Club Red – Short Stories
ddy's Dare – Knox and Summer
Sold to my Ex's Dad - Evan and Jana
Jingling His Bells – Zion and Emma

Club Red: Chicago
Elusive Dom

Chasing the Sun Duet
Sunrise – Kade and Lin
Sunset – Jasper and Brynn

Rock Stars of Nashville
She's Still The One – Dallas and Austin

Standalone Books
Texting Titan - Denver and Avery
Accidental Sugar Daddy – Owen and Ellie
Stay With Me Now – David and Ivy
Midnight Rose - Ruby and Orlando
Committed Cowboy – Whiskey Run Cowboys
Stalking His Obsession - Dakota and Grant
Falling in Love on Route 66 - Weston and Rory
Billionaire's Marigold - Mari and Dalton
A Baby for Her Best Friend – Nick and Summer

CONNECT WITH KACI ROSE

Website
Facebook
Kaci Rose Reader's Facebook Group
TikTok
Instagram
Twitter
Goodreads
Book Bub
Join Kaci Rose's VIP List (Newsletter)

ABOUT KACI ROSE

Kaci Rose writes steamy contemporary romance mostly set in small towns. She grew up in Florida but longs for the mountains over the beach.

She is a mom to 5 kids and a dog who is scared of his own shadow.

She also writes steamy cowboy romance as Kaci M. Rose.

PLEASE LEAVE A REVIEW!

I love to hear from my readers! Please **head over to your favorite store and leave a review** of what you thought of this book!

Made in the USA
Columbia, SC
23 September 2024